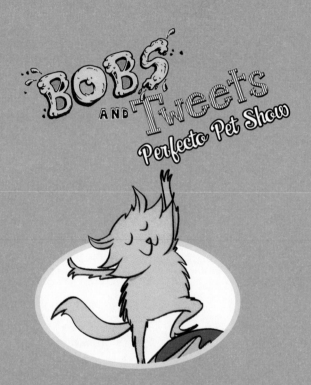

READ MORE

BOBS AND Tweets

BOOKS!

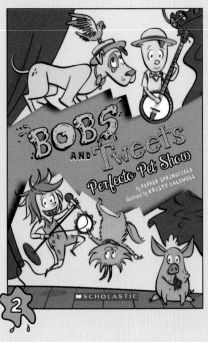

BOBS AND Tweets

Perfecto Pet Show

by PEPPER SPRINGFIELD

illustrated by KRISTY CALDWELL

SCHOLASTIC INC.

For J.E.M.
–PS

For my favorite slob. She knows who she is.
–KC

Library of Congress Cataloging-in-Publication Data

Names: Springfield, Pepper, author. | Caldwell, Kristy, illustrator. | Springfield, Pepper. Bobs and Tweets; #2.
Title: Perfecto pet show / by Pepper Springfield; illustrated by Kristy Caldwell.
Description: First edition. | New York: Scholastic Inc., 2017. | Series: Bobs and Tweets; #2 | Summary: Bonefish School is having a pet talent show and the parents are all invited—but Dean Bob is worried because the other members of his family are such slobs, and Lou Tweet is embarrassed because her family cannot show up anywhere without wanting to start cleaning, and the two families are always at odds with each other.
Identifiers: LCCN 2016041729 | ISBN 9780545870733 (hardcover)
Subjects: LCSH: Pet shows—Juvenile fiction. | Neighbors—Juvenile fiction. | Interpersonal conflict—Juvenile fiction. | Families—Juvenile fiction. | Elementary schools—Juvenile fiction. | Stories in rhyme. | CYAC: Stories in rhyme. | Pet shows—Fiction. | Neighbors—Fiction. | Family life—Fiction. | Schools—Fiction.
Classification: LCC PZ7.1.S717 Pe 2017 | DDC [E]—dc23 LC record available at https://lccn.loc.gov/2016041729

10 9 8 7 6 5 4 3 2 1   17 18 19 20 21

Printed in the U.S.A.   88
First edition, July 2017

Book design by Becky James

TABLE OF CONTENTS

CHAPTER 1
(ALMOST) LATE FOR SCHOOL

Lou Tweet is dancing outside with her cat

While she waits for Dean Bob, that boy with the hat.

They need to leave soon. School starts at eight.

But today, Lou's friend Dean is running quite late.

"Are you done yet?" asks Lou. "Almost ready!" cries Dean.
"Chopper needs one more rinse to make sure he is clean.
My Bobs had a food fight with cold mac and cheese.
Does my dog still smell cheesy? Can you sniff his fur, please?"

"I love food fights," says Lou. "When is the next?
I will rush over. Just send me a text.
We do not have food fights. Never. Not one.
My Tweets are allergic to rowdy, loud fun."

"Just like me!" Dean Bob sighs. "Food fights cause me stress.
I do not play with food. I clean up my mess.
I really adore them, my six other Bobs.
But sometimes I wish they were not such big slobs."

Dean packs up his scrub brush. He rolls up the hose.
He wipes cheddar cheese from between Chopper's toes.
"Thanks for waiting—and sniffing—I am ready at last.
We can make it to school on time if we walk fast."

CHAPTER 2
MS. PAT'S BIG NEWS

It is 8:03 when they get to their class.

"Oh no," groans Dean Bob. "We will need a late pass."

But today no one minds when they walk through the door.

All the kids in Ms. Pat's class are in an uproar.

The kids gape at Ms. Pat as they take their seats.
She is holding identical green parakeets.
"Class, meet my six pets: The twins, Andy and Sandy.
Pippi, my piglet. My iguana named Mandy.

In the tank on the table is Neil, my pet eel."
(As Ms. Pat is talking, Pippi lets out a squeal.)
"Napping under Zach's desk is my cat, Donald Crews.
My pets are here with me to share some Big News.

We are holding our school's first Kid-Pet Talent Show!
Now I will tell you what you need to know.

Pick out a fun act to perform with your pet.
Do magic. Tell jokes. Play a kid-pet duet.
Show off your talent. Dance. Sing a song.
Your act should be no more than three minutes long.

If you have a real pet, please let me know.
But all kinds of creatures can be in our show.
Make-believe pets will work just fine, too.
Or I can loan one of my six pets to you.

Neil, or Mandy, or my cat, Donald Crews,
Can be your pet partner on the act that you choose.
Sing with Andy and Sandy. Tell jokes to my pig.
Pippi loves to dress up. She looks great in a wig.

Our show is next Saturday at half past noon.
Just ten days from now. So start practicing soon.
Be at school by twelve noon. Your folks must come, too,
To show their support for our class and for you.

Take home this flyer to share our Big News."
"Oh no," sighs Dean Bob. "I wish I could refuse.
My Bobs will be rowdy. Noisy. Not cool.
I worry so much when my Bobs come to school."

"I know just what you mean. I get it," says Lou.
"I feel exactly the same way as you.
My Tweets will come early on the day of the show
And insist they get six clean seats in the front row."

The rest of the school day goes by in a blur.

Chucky gets gum stuck in Donald Crews's fur.

Ms. Pat gives a pop quiz. The whole class scores quite low.

The kids have their minds on one thing: The Pet Show.

CHAPTER 3
LOU STANDS ON HER CHAIR

The Tweets have their supper at six on the dot.
Each Tweet takes a seat, always in the same spot.
As they pick up their forks, Lou stands on her chair.
"Tweets, listen! I have some Big School News to share.

Ms. Pat brought her six pets to school today.
To announce our class Pet Show next Saturday.
Pretty Kitty and I will be stars in the show
And all of my Tweets are expected to go."

"Yippee-yee!" peep the Tweets. "We know what you can do.
A live cooking demo of our Good-for-You Stew.
We can all croon smooth jazz tunes and play clarinet.
Or dance *The Nutcracker* while you pirouette.

We can give you flute lessons. You can learn violin.
Just let us know when we should begin."
"No, thank you," says Lou. "It is under control.
Pretty Kitty and I sing old-school rock 'n' roll."

CHAPTER 4
DEAN HAS A TUMMY ACHE

At the Bobs' house, Chef Bob makes a juicy pig roast.
Dean's tummy feels funny. He just wants tea and toast.
"Bobs, listen," says Dean. "I am in a class show
For kids and their pets. Ms. Pat wants you to go."

"Whoop! Whoop!" the Bobs cheer. "A kid-pet show sounds cool.
We love it when we get to go to your school.
We are Bobs-at-the-Ready to give you a hand.
We can teach you new tricks. Back you up with our band."

"No, thank you," says Dean as he pats Chopper's head.
"I have picked out a banjo number instead."
"Perfecto!" whoops Bob Two. "We can all learn that song.
Then all of your Bobs, we can all sing along."

23

"Please, Bobs," whispers Dean, "do the best thing for *me*.
Just get there on time and behave politely."
He goes to the fridge and hangs up Ms. Pat's flyer,
Then wipes up some grease from the Bobs' deep fat fryer.

CHAPTER 5
BIKE LANE

Saturday of the Pet Show dawns sunny and bright,
But the kids in Ms. Pat's class were up half the night.
They are nervous. And worried. Performing is tough.
Did they practice their acts for the show well enough?

Six Tweets never, ever want to be late.

Tweet One has their bikes ready at half past eight.

Lou says, "Hey, Tweets! I should be there at noon.

We really do not need to leave home so soon.

My Bonefish Street School is ten minutes away.

Trust me. It is close. I go there every day."

"We are leaving right *now*," six Tweets peep to Lou.

"There is a lot of hard work we Tweets need to do.

We will damp mop the floor. Try to freshen the air.
Spray sanitizer and wipe down each chair.
We want to meet all your friends and chat with Ms. Pat.
And be sure to wash our hands well after that.

We need to set up our cameras. Get the best view.
To make sure we can film Pretty Kitty and you.
We want to save six clean seats in the front row.
Come on, Lou, it really is time to go."

Down Bonefish Street, the Tweets ride in a line.

Everything seems to be going just fine

When the Tweets turn the corner past the streetlamp.

Then, there, out of nowhere, is a huge skateboard ramp.

Tweet One's front bike wheel gets caught on the edge.
Then—*uh-oh!*—she crashes down over the ledge.
The six other Tweets, they all start to tumble.
All of them falling, their bikes in a jumble.

31

Tweets are bruised. They are dirty. Their bikes are a wreck.
Pretty Kitty has mud in the fur on her neck.
"Who will help us?" Tweets wail. "What a terrible fate.
Who made this? A half-pipe? Now we will be late!"

The Tweets are indignant. That means they are MAD.
Who on Bonefish Street would do something so BAD?

CHAPTER 6
ROAD RAGE!

Dean and Chopper are strumming in Dean's room alone
When Dean sees an emergency text on his phone.
We Tweets had a crash. Please help. This is Lou.
Can you call someone quickly to do a rescue?

Dean runs down the stairs. Chopper lets out a yelp.
"WAKE UP, Bobs!" screams Dean. "My friend Lou needs our help."
Bob One blows the foghorn he keeps by his side.
"Team Bob: First Responders: Let's go take a ride!"

Bob One drives the van, FAST, down the street.

He spots fourteen pairs of Tweet hands and Tweet feet.

"It looks like those Tweets took a really bad spill."

"Are you sure?" asks Bob Two. "It could be roadkill."

"No way!" yells Bob Three. "Bobs, check out my side.
Those seven neat Tweets had a nasty, rough ride.
Their bikes are tipped over. Each wheel has a dent.
Their red handlebars are all twisted and bent."

"Whoop! Whoop!" hoots Bob Six from the top of the bus.
"Hey, Bobs! Those Tweets are skaters like us!"

The Bob Van pulls up to the accident site.
"Lou," shouts Dean Bob. "Are you Tweets all alright?"
Before Dean can even step out of the van,
Six Tweets are peeping as loud as they can.

"Was it YOU Bobs who built this huge skateboard ramp?
This is our street. It is not X-Games camp.
This ramp is a hazard. So dangerous, too.
How could you think this was okay to do?"

"Now, hold on," the Bobs cry. "We live here to have fun.
We Bobs need to have a good, fast skateboard run.
We can practice our ollies and work on our flips.
Next time you try it, we will give you some tips."

"There WILL NOT be a next time. This ramp must come down
Or all of you Bobs must move out of this town."
"Uh . . . NO WAY!" yell the Bobs. "That is not true.
Bonefish Street is for fun. Not for spoilsports like you."

"STOP!" Lou Tweet shouts. "Put your fighting aside."
"Bobs!" Dean Bob pleads. "We must give them a ride.
It is getting so late. We will miss our pet show.
Stop fighting now, all of you. We need to go."

So the Tweets pile in with their bikes and their gear.
They sit in the front. The Bobs move to the rear.
Bob One drives the Bob Van as fast as it goes.
Six unhappy Tweets are each holding their nose.

At 12:20 the Bob Van pulls in the school drive.

"We are here," peep the Tweets. "We are here and alive."

"Phew," says Ms. Pat. "I was starting to worry.

Please take your seats. Come on now. Let's hurry."

CHAPTER 7

THE FIRST EVER BONEFISH STREET SCHOOL KID-PET TALENT SHOW

Ms. Pat climbs on stage in front of the crowd.

"Welcome to all. Today I am so proud.

I have a class full of talented students this year.

As their teacher, I am thrilled that you are all here."

Ms. Pat continues, "I have one strict rule.
We are very good sports at Bonefish Street School.
Please cheer for each act. Make each student feel good.
Show Bonefish Street pride in our school neighborhood.

We welcome all kids with their pets, real or not.
We believe every student deserves their best shot.

We have four special guests sitting in the front row.
Community leaders you should get to know:

From Police Headquarters, welcome Captain Jo'leen.
Mo, Bonefish Street's Mayor, is here on the scene.
Meet Mark, our cool lifeguard from the Bonefish Street Pool.
Please greet Mr. Fred Bigtree, the heart of our school."

The four special guests stand up, wave, and grin.
"Okay," says Ms. Pat. "Let the Pet Show begin."

Brea goes first with her bunny named Sunny.
They perform magic tricks that are pretty funny.
"Shazam!" Brea says. Sunny hops in a hat.
Then Sunny hops out again, dressed as a cat.

"Whoop! Whoop!" the Bobs cheer. "Go, Brea! Go, Sunny.
Awesome! We love it! That is one funny bunny."
The crowd cheers and applauds for Brea T. Lee.
The Tweets in the second row peep politely.

Sherman O'Leary does not have a pet.

He chose to perform with his sister, Yvette.

Yvette is wearing a brown hamster suit.

"Whoop! Whoop!" yell six Bobs. "That hamster is cute."

BONEFISH STREET SCHOOL KID-PET TALENT SHOW

Samir G. goes next. He does tricks with his beagle.
Then Ramona Diaz flies her remote-control eagle.
The Tweets clap softly—they hate to be loud.
The Bobs in the back holler like a huge crowd.

Ms. Pat introduces the next boy, named Zach.

He pulls out two creatures from his green fanny pack.

"Meet my frog and my toad. Please take a close look.

They will act out a scene from my favorite book."

The kids take their turns. The acts go pretty well.
Only Chucky Parnell ran too fast and fell.
He was dancing with Pippi and Donald Crews
When he tripped on the laces of his brand-new school shoes.

"Chopper," Dean whispers, "our turn will come soon.
I have such a bad feeling I will play out of tune.
I want this show to be over. I know I will freeze.
I cannot seem to steady my wobbly knees."

CHAPTER 8
DEAN AND LOU TAKE THE STAGE

"Now Dean Bob," says Ms. Pat, "and Chopper, his pet,
Will perform an original boy-dog duet."
"Go, Dean! Go, Chopper! Whoop! Whoop!" the Bobs cheer.
"Sing it loud! Sing it proud! We all want to hear."

Dean Bob takes his banjo and he starts to strum.

But he is too nervous. He cannot even hum.

Chopper is howling and doing his best,

But Dean Bob cannot sing. His heart thumps in his chest.

Lou Tweet is backstage. She sees her friend's plight.
"Pretty Kitty!" she yells. "Enter stage right!"
Lou grabs the mic and says, "Folks, listen up.
Pretty Kitty and I will join Dean and his pup."

Lou whispers to Dean, "Just play what you know.
We will follow along. It will be a great show."

Dean Bob plays one note and looks over at Lou.
He feels a bit better. Lou knows what to do.
"Pretty Kitty," Lou says, "and Chopper, let's groove.
Let's show this audience how we can move."

Dean strums his banjo. Everyone claps along.

At the end of the act, the crowd yells, "ONE MORE SONG!"

"You saved me," says Dean as they do an encore.

"No problemo," says Lou. "That is what friends are for."

"Okay," says Ms. Pat. "That concludes our Pet Show.
Just wait one more minute before you get up to go.
Please stay in your seats while our guests file through.
They will pose on the red carpet for photos with you."

Captain Jo'leen says, "We guests all agree,
Mayor Mo, Lifeguard Mark, Mr. Bigtree, and me,
Your students are great, such a talented crew.
They are lucky, Ms. Pat, that their teacher is you."

"Yippee-yee!" peep the Tweets. "Such a wonderful bunch."
"Perfecto!" yell the Bobs. "Is it time for lunch?"
The crowd goes wild. They clap their hands and they cheer.
"This Pet Show was great. We cannot wait for next year!"

NEXT WEEK:
"LIFE IS A DREAM"
A PLAY IN THREE ACTS

CHAPTER 9
TIME TO GO

After red-carpet photos and punch and a snack,
The showgoers make their way out the back.
The Tweets hear a shout as they walk through the door.
"I fixed up your bikes! Surprise!" yells Bob Four.

"I unbent your fenders and inflated your tires.
I oiled your kickstands, fixed your gears with new wires.
Plus, each bike now has Wi-Fi and a Blurpee cupholder.
And faux fur–covered seats for when the weather gets colder."

"Oh no," gasps Dean Bob. "What will the Tweets say?
Bob Four fixed the Tweets' bikes the Bob-fashioned way."

Dean covers his ears. He shuts his eyes tight.

He thinks: "Here comes another Bobs versus Tweets fight."

But he exhales with relief when the Tweets peep, "Thanks, Bob.

You really did quite an excellent job."

"Tweets!" Tweet Four peeps. "These Bobs really helped us.

Let's repay the favor and clean out their bus."

So the Tweets go to work scrubbing out the Bob Van.

They clean and they wipe till it shines spick-and-span.

"Let's go wait on the swings," Lou says to Dean.
"We have to stay out of Tweets' way while they clean."
Lou practices wheelies on her bike's super tires
As Mo and the Ruckers hand out "VOTE FOR MO" flyers.

It takes a good hour, but the Bob Van is clean.
Bob Five says with respect, "You Tweets are a machine."
Bob Three hoots, "WOW! You found Chopper's first collar
And our special gold-plated Bobs' souvenir dollar!"

At last, at the end of this long Saturday,
Six Bobs and six Tweets all go their own way.
Lou Tweet and Dean Bob decide they will walk
Like they do every day, and continue to talk.

"Tomorrow," says Dean, "we have things we can do.
Tweet Two invited me over for Good-for-You Stew.
I want to practice banjo so I will be ready
For the next talent show, train my nerves to be steady.

"We can go to the library on Dolphin Road
To check out Zach's book about the frog and the toad.
In the afternoon we can chill out and read
And have some relaxing downtime, which we need."

I want to hang out with you," Lou says to Dean.
"But I am not allowed out until my room is clean."
"No offense, Lou," says Dean. "But your room *is* quite dirty.
I will come help you clean it. Let's start at eight thirty."

So Lou Tweet and Dean Bob and both of their pets
Walk home, trying out new kid-pet quartets.
"Dean, remember," says Lou, as she hugs her cat tight,
"When we stick together, things work out just right."

THE END

PEPPER SPRINGFIELD

Pepper was born and raised in Massachusetts. Pepper loves rock 'n' roll and chocolate, just like Lou Tweet. And like Dean Bob, Pepper loves to read and do crossword puzzles. Over the years, Pepper has loved all kinds of pets: dogs, cats, hamsters, turtles, fish, a bunny, and an imaginary monkey. Pepper does not like the spotlight. pepperspringfield.com

KRISTY CALDWELL

Kristy received an MFA in illustration from the School of Visual Arts. She is a full-time illustrator and a part-time Tweet. While working at her art studio in Brooklyn, New York, Kristy gets her creativity on like Lou Tweet, drinks tea like Dean Bob, and hangs out with her energetic dog friend, Dutch. kristycaldwell.com